THE GOOD SON

A Story from the First World War,
Told in Miniature

PIERRE-JACQUES OBER

illustrated by JULES OBER *and* FELICITY COONAN

CANDLEWICK STUDIO
an imprint of Candlewick Press

About one hundred years ago, the whole world went to war.

The war was supposed to last months.

It lasted years.

The first Christmas approached, came, and passed.

Everyone struggled to stay warm.

Soldiers marched to battle once again.

Except one.

Pierre was locked up inside a barn.

"What's going on in there?"

"Pierre deserted. He was gone for two days.
When he came back this morning, they locked him up."

"I hope you enjoyed Christmas at home."
"Why did you come back?"

Pierre was quiet.

"Here comes your friend Gilbert."

Gilbert, strange Gilbert, had brought Pierre bread, butter, wine, and, for a moment, warmth.

"What will happen to Pierre?"   "I'd say he's in big trouble."

Pierre was left alone to await his fate.

Surely the fact that I returned after two days will lessen the sentence. . . . The lieutenant will put in a good word for me.

In August 1914, I signed up to fight like everyone else.

I saw the posters; I answered the call.

I wanted to make my mother proud.

The whole country felt the same way.

We wanted to stop the Germans. We wanted to stop the awful things they were doing.

Quatrième année. — N° 40.   Le Numéro : **25** centimes.   DIMANCHE 30 août 1914.

LE MIROIR

PUBLICATION HEBDOMADAIRE, 18, Rue d'Enghien, PARIS

LE MIROIR paie n'importe quel prix les documents photographiques relatifs à la guerre, présentant un intérêt particulier.

Les ATROCITES ALLEMANDES en Belgique

LES ALLEMANDS SEMENT LA DESTRUCTION SUR LEUR PASSAGE

DES MILLIERS DE CIVILS SANS ABRIS

C'est un soldat que l'on aurait jugé de loin sur sa silhouette toujours haute, mais qui, une fois approché, ouvrant sa capote, vous montrerait sa poitrine déchirée. Les pierres se détachent d'elle. Une maladie la désagrège. Une horrible main l'a écorchée vive.

So we marched all over the countryside.

It was beautiful.

I was part of something bigger than myself. We all were.

We all dreamed of glory.

Then we finally saw battle.

We won.

It was terrible.

I began to keep to myself. I felt doubtful and alone.

Alone, except for Gilbert, strange Gilbert.
He was always close by—watching over me. He would put himself between me and the bullets.

In September, we saw action once more. We fought alongside the Zouaves, our comrades from North Africa.

At the height of the battle, I found myself surrounded. Then Gilbert arrived.

Gilbert saved me. He was fearless.

"Pierre! The colonel is coming!"

"Attention!"

"Soldier, you left the regiment without orders for two days.
Despite your return this morning and your good record, this is unacceptable.

"Tomorrow, you will be shot for desertion.
Soldier, I do not salute you."

About one hundred years ago, the whole world went to war.

They called it the Great War, but it was fought by little soldiers.

Pierre wished he could speak to his mother, back home. But he couldn't.

So he spoke to the moon.

He told the moon he wanted to fall in love, to get married, to have a baby girl . . .

and show her Paris.

But the moon could not hear him. It was too far away.

So Pierre began to climb.

That was the moment his lieutenant came to say goodbye.

"High Command is very worried about the morale of the army, worried more men will walk away.
They said the war would be over by Christmas, and it's not.

"The colonel has decided to make an example of you."

"There's nothing I can do."

"If you try to escape, they will catch you and your family will be shamed. Be brave."

Pierre decided to write to his mother.

Chère Maman,

I don't know how I'll get this letter
to you, but I know I will be dead by
the time you read it. I'm so sorry for
the pain I am causing you. It breaks
my heart. Since Father died, we only
have each other, and all I ever wanted
was to make you happy and proud.

I left to spend Christmas with you
because I wanted to be a good son,
and I returned to the regiment because
I wanted to remain a good soldier.

I thought I was doing the right
thing. Now it feels like the world
has gone mad.

Let me tell you something that
happened in September.

I was sent on a scouting mission to find water at a nearby well.
When I got to the farm, I found a group of Germans sitting around a fire.

When they saw me, they stood—and we all froze.
Then one of them raised an arm and asked, "Kaffee, Kamerad?"

They offered me a seat. I joined them. They could speak some French.
I could speak a little bit of German— do you remember teaching me some words?

One offered me chocolate. They were all dressed in gray.
My pants and hat were red. But otherwise . . .

They were tired, too.

They were tired of marching, of sleeping outside, tired of backpack sores and boot blisters. Tired of being away from their families.

They weren't huge and scary like I'd been told. We were all just little soldiers caught up in a big mess.

Then they told me about their last attack. On us.

We'd beaten them.

It was terrible.

I was astounded. We all felt the same way.
War was no different for them.

They said they were resting there—hiding actually. They'd had enough killing.
They asked me to take them prisoner. To take them back to my regiment. So I did.

Why am I telling you this?

I was commended by the colonel for having taken six prisoners, when, in fact, I should have been shot for fraternizing with the enemy. And now I will be shot for desertion, when, in fact, I returned.

I didn't want you to be alone for Christmas, and now I'll be leaving you alone for good. None of it makes sense.

But what a Christmas it was! I came like Père Noël bearing gifts, and we lit the tree and talked and laughed.

I'll wear my new socks tomorrow. You'll keep me warm. Maman, those were the best two days of the war.

I love you.

Pierre

Joyeux
Noël
Maman

Merry
Christmas
Pierre

Just before dawn, Gilbert came back.

He brought bread, butter, wine, warmth.

"You have always looked after me, Gilbert. Now I have to ask you—why?"

"I had a little brother once. He was like you — good, eager to please, perhaps a little too smart for his own good. He was killed the first week of the war. He was also too young to die."

Pierre told him about the letter he'd written to his mother.

Gilbert made a promise.

About one hundred years ago, the whole world went to war.

It was supposed to last months.

It was supposed to be over by Christmas.

It was fought by little soldiers like Pierre.

It would be won by little soldiers like Pierre.

But not by Christmas. And not by Pierre.

I was born into a military family. History and little soldiers have always been integral parts of my life. As a child, I was lulled by bugle calls, by the music and songs of martial parades. My father was an officer, so as we moved from one military posting to the next, from Algeria to Berlin and all over France, I was constantly surrounded by men in uniform, by army trucks, tanks, and cannons.

As early as I can remember, I loved to escape into imaginary worlds. Either playing with little soldiers in my room or dressing up to re-create epic battles and heroic deeds on my own in our yard.

My hyperactive imagination was fired up by the stories told by my maternal grandfather. A military equestrian master, he was a tough romantic who would bow to no one but had no shame in crying when evoking war, listening to music, or reciting poetry. His stories were full of historical heroes, adventurers, honor, and bravery. I owe to him my romantic soul and my idealistic nature.

The year 2014 corresponded to my father's eightieth birthday and to the centenary of the start of World War I.

As a gift, I decided to make a series of images of my World War I figurines in memory of my paternal grandfather—a highly decorated soldier of the Great War. He died before I was born, worn out by decades of constant warfare.

My father is now eighty-five, and the personal project in memory of a grandfather I never knew has developed into an homage to all the men who fulfilled their patriotic duty unprepared for the horror unleashed upon them. I tell the stories of the "little soldiers" who submitted to dramatic events far beyond their control, to better understand their true heroism: the way they retained their humanity amid it all.

I didn't follow the military family tradition. I preferred philosophy, music, and films. But in playing with the metaphor of the "little soldier" while using photography to portray a period during which that medium came of age, I found a way to get closer to these young men and some of what they may have felt.

Pierre-Jacques Ober

Contrary to traditional storytelling methods, in which a story is first imagined and written, then brought to life with drawings or with actors, animation, or CGI, we decided to make a story from preexisting materials: models and miniatures available at hobby shops around the world. That way it felt as if the "little soldiers" themselves were telling us their stories. The story was drawn from them instead of them being used to suit the purpose of a pre-written story.

Overcoming the restrictions and limitations associated with creating and telling a story in such an unusual way has been the first creative challenge of this process.

A second challenge was how we could bring emotion to our very stiff and expressionless little plastic men—how to create an eerie reality that would take the viewer beyond their plastic edges to feel and share with them the terrible array of emotions they experience. Credit for overcoming this challenge goes to the emotional power of the photography. The use of framing, depth of field, the decision to use only natural light at different times of day, and the very important step of making digital adjustments to color and texture all helped us not only to capture an emotion with each image but also to create an overall feeling for the story.

This book has been created by following a process similar to that used in filmmaking, but in miniature.

The authors would like to thank
William Callahan, Wendy Harper,
Jacques and Jacqueline Ober,
and Elaine Lewis.

Text copyright © 2019 by Pierre-Jacques Ober
Photographs copyright © 2019 by Jules Ober

First U.S. edition 2019

Library of Congress Catalog Card Number 2018962035
ISBN 978-1-5362-0482-7

19 20 21 22 23 24 LEO 10 9 8 7 6 5 4 3 2 1

Printed in Heshan, Guangdong, China

This book was typeset in Caslon.

Candlewick Studio
an imprint of
Candlewick Press
99 Dover Street
Somerville, Massachusetts 02144

www.candlewickstudio.com